BANG! BOOM! ROAR!

A Busy Crew of Dinosaurs

TYRANNOSAURUS REX

(tye-ran-uh-SAWR-us recks)

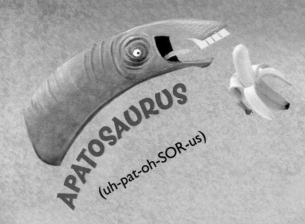

APATOSAURUS

(uh-pat-oh-SOR-us)

COMPSOGNATHUS

(komp-sug-NAY-thus)

TRICERATOPS

(try-SAIR-uh-tops)

STEGOSAURUS

(steg-uh-SAWR-us)

PINACOSAURUS

(pin-uh-kuh-SAWR-us)

EUOPLOCEPHALUS

(you-op-luh-SEF-uh-lus)

PSITTACOSAURUS

(SIT-uh-ko-sawr-us)

PROTOCERATOPS

(pro-toe-SAIR-uh-tops)

STRUTHIOMIMUS

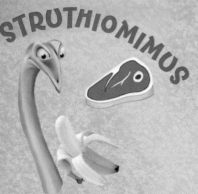

(stroo-thee-oh-MIE-mus)

ANKYLOSAURUS

(ang-kile-uh-SAWR-us)

HADROSAURUS

(HAD-ruh-sawr-us)

CAMARASAURUS
(kam-uh-ruh-SOR-us)

PTERANODON
(te-RAN-oh-don)

PACHYCEPHALOSAURUS
(pak-ee-SEF-uh-lo-sawr-us)

ALBERTOSAURUS
(al-ber-tuh-SAWR-us)

PARASAUROLOPHUS
(par-uh-SAWR-ah-loh-fus)

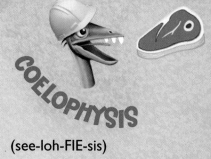

COELOPHYSIS
(see-loh-FIE-sis)

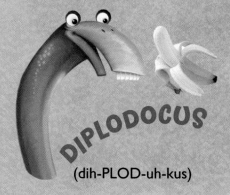

DIPLODOCUS
(dih-PLOD-uh-kus)

IGUANODON
(ig-WAN-oh-don)

ANATOSAURUS
(uh-nat-oh-SOR-us)

CENTROSAURUS
(sen-truh-SAWR-us)

= MEAT EATER

= PLANT EATER

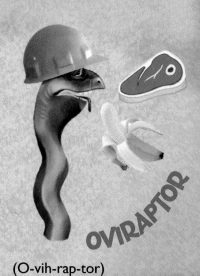

OVIRAPTOR
(O-vih-rap-tor)

To my darling, Prentiss. I miss you so much. You're forever in my heart.
Thank you to all the wonderful doctors, nurses, and staff
at the Mayo Clinic and Dana-Farber Cancer Institute. You are all heroes.
My love and appreciation to all Prentiss's and my family and friends
who supported us in so many ways and with so much kindness.
And thanks to Stephanie, Caryn, Phoebe, and Chris for helping to build this book.
—N.E.

Dedicated to the memory of my mother: her wit, tenacious spirit, and voice
—S.G.B.

For Jamie
—C.S.

ISBN 978-0-545-62381-0

Text copyright © 2012 by Nate Evans and Stephanie Gwyn Brown.
Illustrations copyright © 2012 by Christopher Santoro.
All rights reserved. Published by Scholastic Inc., 557 Broadway, New York, NY 10012,
by arrangement with HarperCollins Children's Books, a division of HarperCollins Publishers.
SCHOLASTIC and associated logos are trademarks and/or registered trademarks of Scholastic Inc.

12 11 10 9 8 7 6 5 4 3 2 1   13 14 15 16 17 18/0

Printed in the U.S.A.   40

First Scholastic printing, September 2013

BANG! BOOM! ROAR!

A Busy Crew of Dinosaurs

By **NATE EVANS**
and
STEPHANIE GWYN BROWN

Illustrated by
CHRISTOPHER SANTORO

SCHOLASTIC INC.

Listen to the RRRUMBLE-**ROARRR!**
Wonder what that noise is for?
Hey, look! Here comes a mighty crew!
They have a building job to do!

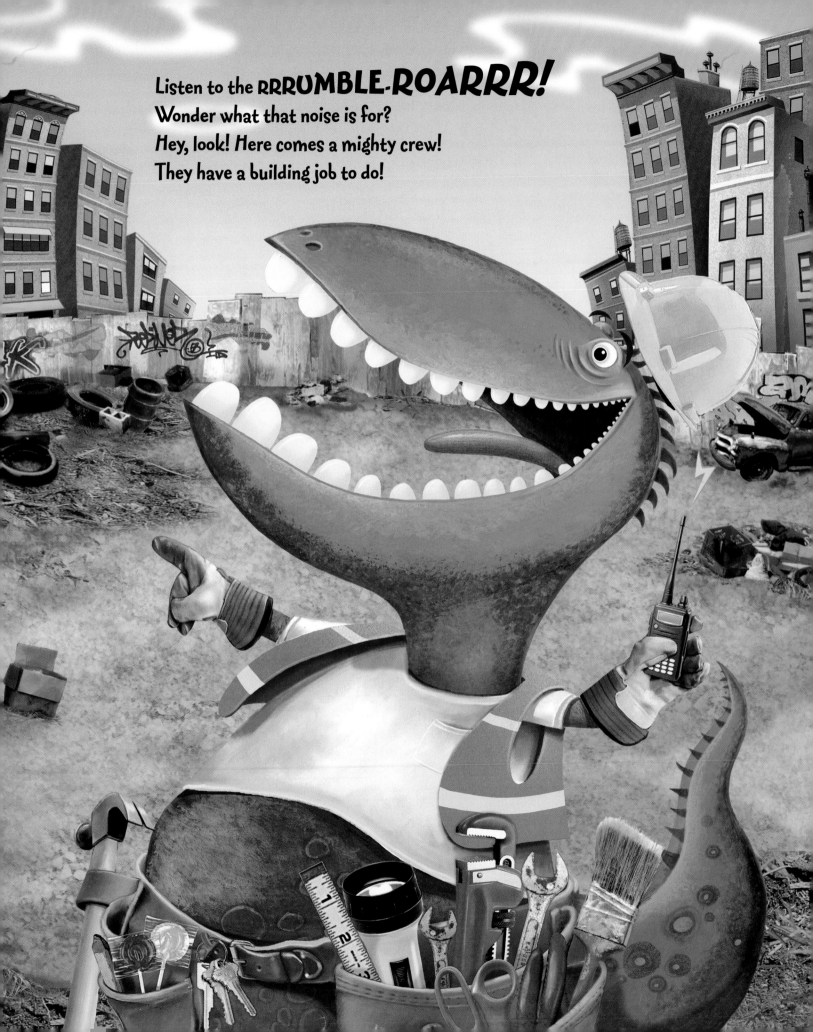

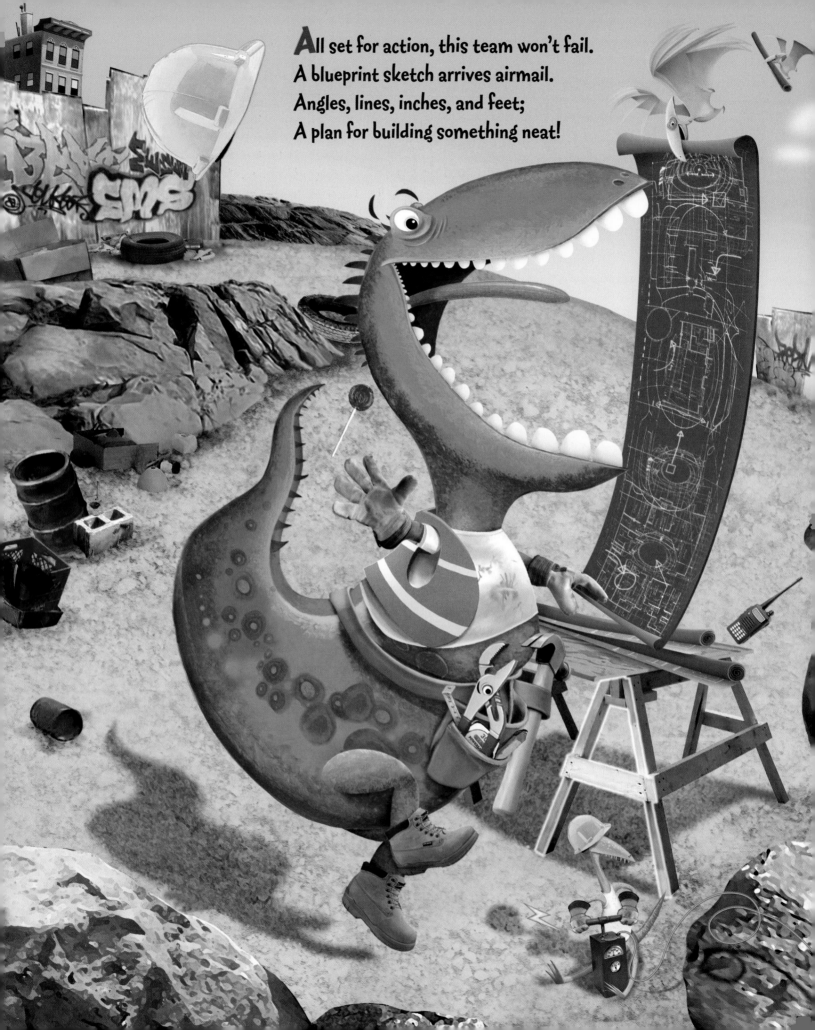

All set for action, this team won't fail.
A blueprint sketch arrives airmail.
Angles, lines, inches, and feet;
A plan for building something neat!

Bulldozers blocked! Can't get across!
"Bust those boulders!" shouts the boss.
Time to use the big bang, BOOM!
Danger! Blasting! Make some room!

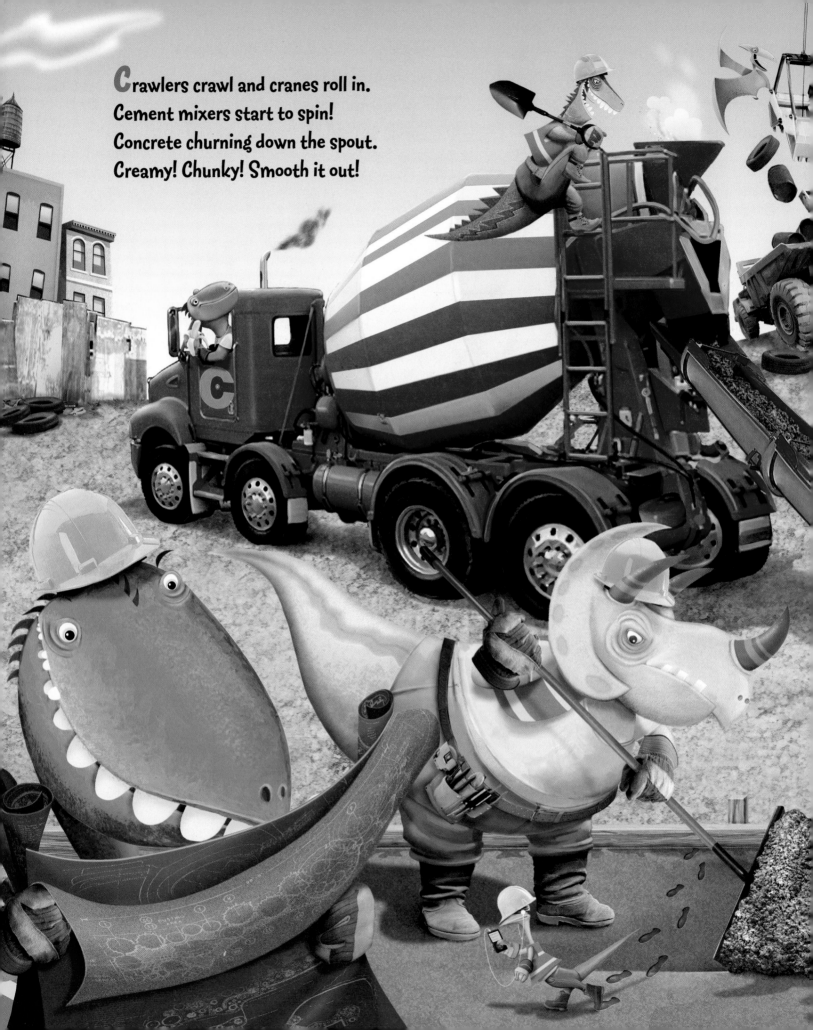

Crawlers crawl and cranes roll in.
Cement mixers start to spin!
Concrete churning down the spout.
Creamy! Chunky! Smooth it out!

Digging, driving, drilling, filling.
Dinos tough and rough and willing.
Dump trucks dumping left, then right.
This dino might use dynamite!

Every engine is in motion.
Excavation, locomotion!
Experts use their elbow grease
To engineer a masterpiece!

Forklifts beeping, shifting freight.
For fitting crates, this fleet's first-rate.
Faster, faster! Four wheels jump!
Freestyle flip-flop! Big speed bump!

Grabber gobbles tons of grit.
Grasping grapple gets a grip.
Grader grinds the ground. Achoo!
Giant sneeze! Green, gunky goo!

ACHOO!

Hard hats, tool belts, heavy boots;
Hammers hanging from their loops.
Heave and hoist! Hydraulic muscle!
Heavy metal, high-wire hustle!

Inspectors check important lists.
"It's safety first," they all insist.
Itsy bitsy words in ink,
Instructions keep the team in sync.

Jackhammers rattle, jolt, and shatter.
Jingle-jangle, clang-bang. CLATTER!
Jelly bellies jump and jiggle.
Jumbo blubber in a wiggle!

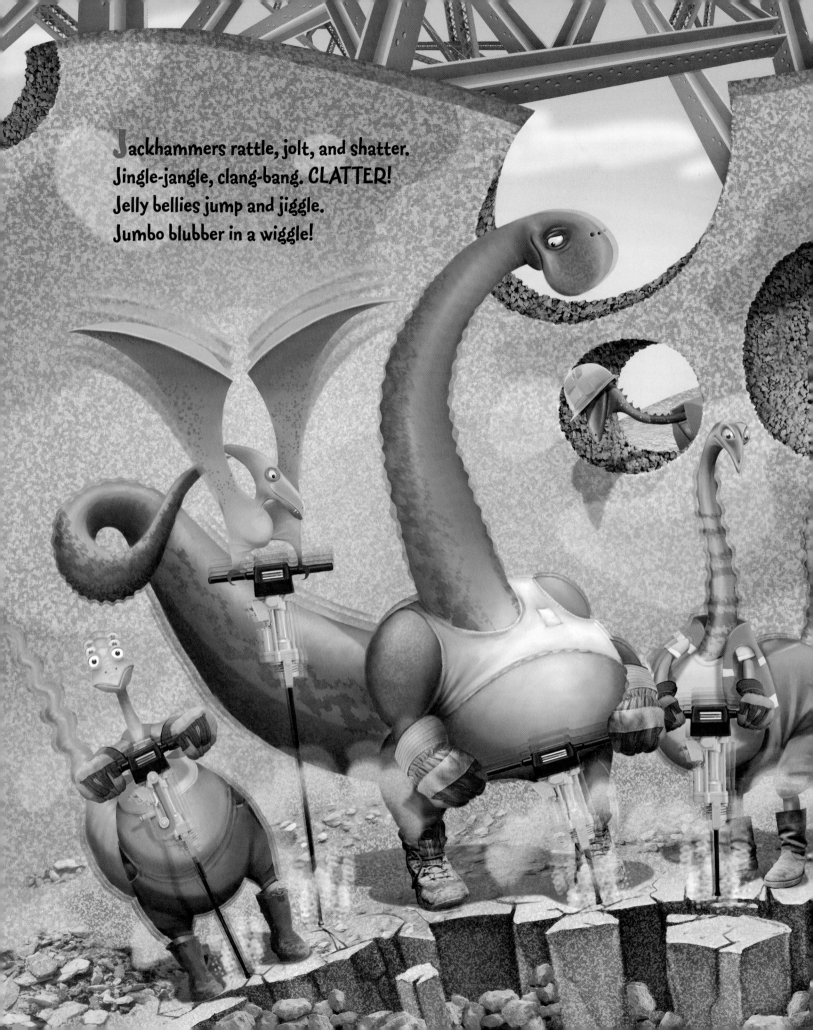

Keypads punched with knack and know-how.
Knobs and levers, crankshaft, GO NOW!
Knock, knock, who's there on those controls?
His backhoe kicks out king-sized holes.

LUNCHTIME! Hear the whistle blow!
Lift those lunchbox lids! Heave-ho!
Liver, lettuce, lemonade.
"I don't like mine. Lemme trade!"

M-m-munch, munch, munch!
Move mounds of lunch!
Their mighty mouths go Slurp! Burp! Crunch!
Mustard squirts make yellow shirts!
Mop your mess and hit the dirt!

Noodle-head, new to the crew.
Shiny name tag, necktie, too.
At pounding nails he's the worst.
OH NO! Ned needs to see the nurse!

One big oil slick Olympic race,
Old wheel loader's in first place!
Knocking over orange cones—
OOPS! Hopping ditches! OUCH!
Flinging stones!

Patch the problems on this project!
Pull together. Make it perfect.
Clean those pipes, please—scoop the goop out.
Come on, plumbers, don't you poop out!

Quartz was hauled in from the quarry.
Carve it quick. They're in a hurry.
Quakes and shakes—a clamoring riot!
When they quit, it will be quiet.

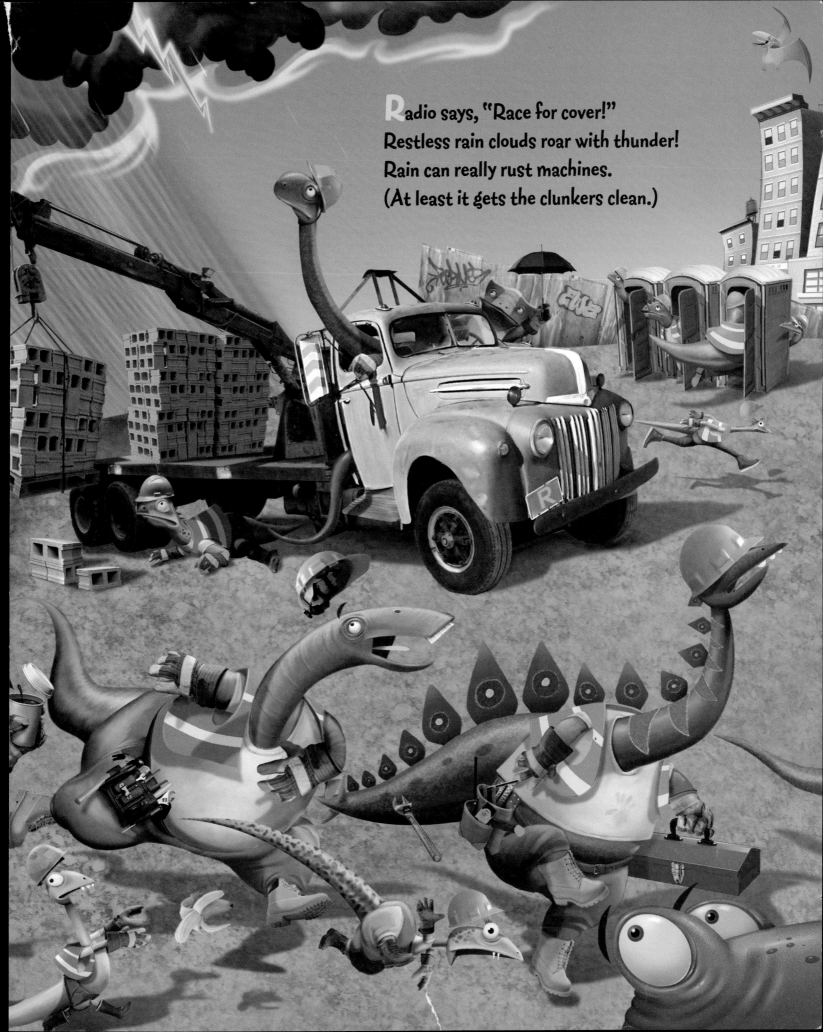

Radio says, "Race for cover!"
Restless rain clouds roar with thunder!
Rain can really rust machines.
(At least it gets the clunkers clean.)

Sunshine dries the swampy muck.
Soon asphalt slides from side dump trucks.
Step it up and stomp the ground.
Steamroller it. Go squish, squash 'round.

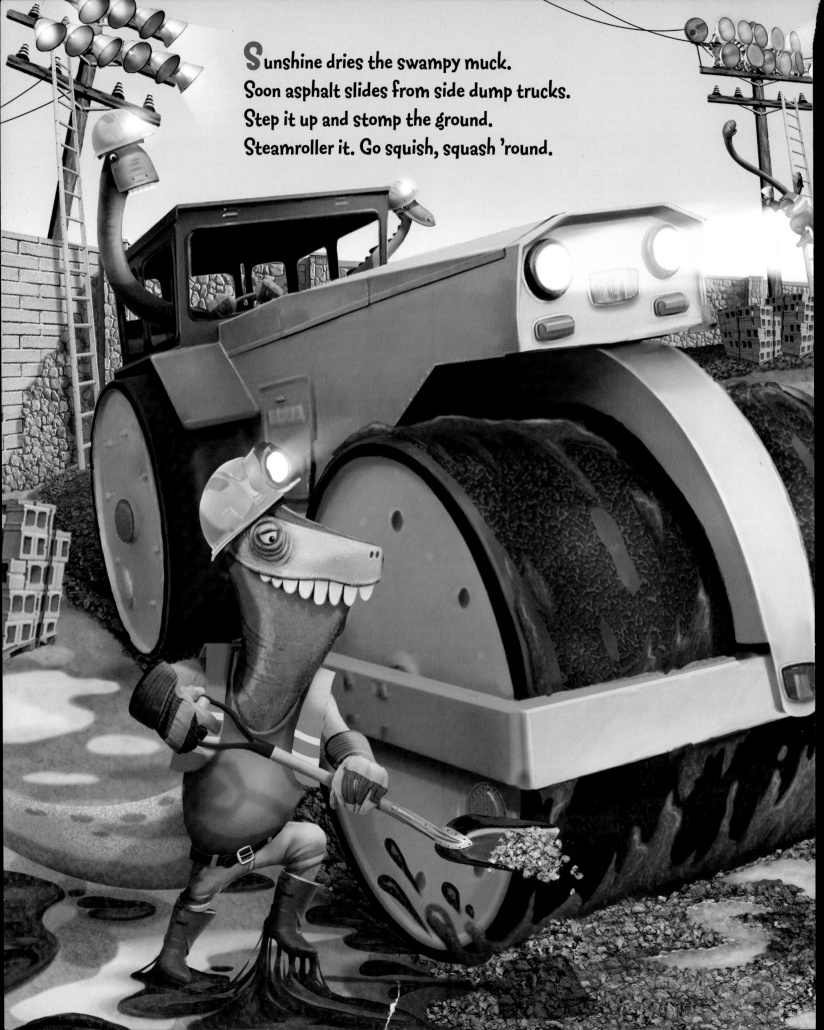

Trample rock with this track paver.
Toss in tar! A true time-saver!
Towering torches and twisting necks.
Teetering, tottering tons of high tech!

Upside-down emergency!
Use a crane with urgency.
Unload. Unpack. No time to spare!
Lift it up—rippp! Underwear!

"**V**-I-C-T-O-R-Y!"
Loud volcano battle cry!
Vapor, lava, venting loose!
Install valves and then vamoose!

Wrenches turning, watch them work.
WHOOOSH! Wild water through the dirt.
Wizards welding final touches.
Whirling, swirling paint with brushes.

X marks the spot to build the exit.
Almost finished. It's quite exquisite!
Exacting work earns extra pay.
Save it for a rainy day.

"You guys did great! You're number one!
"Success! Oh yes," Boss yells. "You're done!"
"Yayyyyyhoorayyyyippeyyyahooo . . ."
Yawns the weary dino crew.

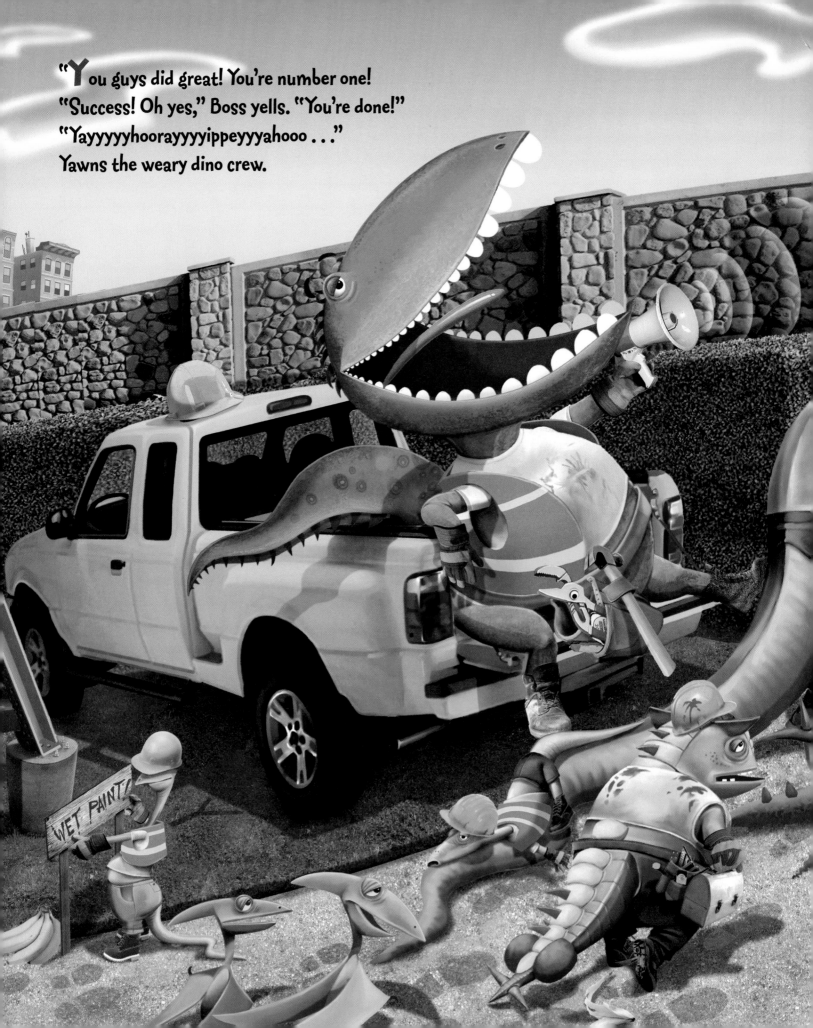

Zigging, zagging, tails dragging.
Dino zest and zip are lagging.
Zonked out—time to catch some
ZZZZZZs.

Lock the gate behind you, please.

Listen to the **RRRUMBLE-ROARRR!**
See now what the noise was for?
The construction site of yesterday
Is now a place for us to play!

CEMENT MIXER

STEAMROLLER

GRABBER

BULLDOZER

WHEEL LOADER

BACKHOE

GRADER

GRAPPLE

DUMP TRUCK

TRACTOR CRANE CRAWLER

JACKHAMMER

SIDE DUMP TRUCK

TRACK PAVER

FORKLIFT

FLATBED TRUCK